JF MADDOX
Maddox, Jake, author.
Blue line breakaway

BLUE LINE BREAKAWAY

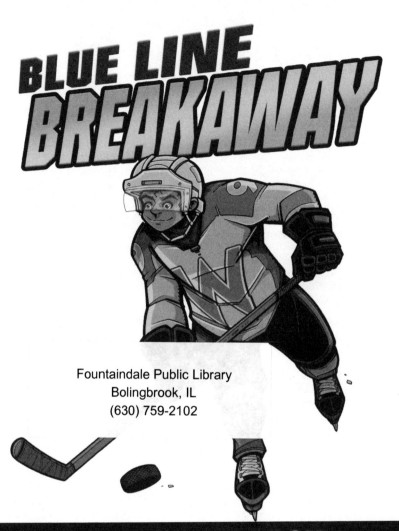

BY JAKE MADDOX

Text by Melissa Brandt
Illustrated by Sean Tiffany

STONE ARCH BOOKS
a capstone imprint

Jake Maddox Sports Stories are published by
Stone Arch Books
a Capstone Imprint
1710 Roe Crest Drive
North Mankato, Minnesota 56003
www.mycapstone.com

Library of Congress Cataloging-in-Publication Data
is available on the Library of Congress website.

ISBN: 978-1-4965-6317-0 (library binding)
ISBN: 978-1-4965-6319-4 (paperback)
ISBN: 978-1-4965-6321-7 (eBook PDF)

Summary: Jack has the talent to be a big-time hockey player—just like
his older sister. Can Jack find a way to slip out of his sister's shadow and
become a hockey phenom in his own right?

Editor: Nate LeBoutillier
Designer: Laura Manthe
Production Specialist: Tori Abraham

Printed in Canada.
PA020

TABLE OF CONTENTS

CHAPTER 1

IN THE DEFENSIVE ZONE

Jack Wickman stepped on the ice and pushed away from the boards. His mouthguard dangled from the corner of his lips. Jack took a few strides toward the bench. Coach Vorwald stood with his hands on his hips behind the glass. Jack couldn't quite look him in the eye.

"You're late, Wickman," Coach Vorwald said.

Jack nodded. "My older sister had a game up north," he said. Jack knew saying that would get him off the hook. Everyone admired his sister.

"Big game coming up," Coach Vorwald said. "Warm up."

Jack scooped one of the pucks off the ice and practiced stickhandling. As he moved the puck toward the blue line, he thought of Becca. Even though his sister was five years older, Jack couldn't help feeling jealous.

Becca's skills were so impressive that coaches had moved her to the boys' team. *Yes*, Jack often said, *Becca's my sister. Yes, she plays hockey on the boys' team.* For some reason, Jack usually had to give the info twice. *Yes, she's my sister. Yes, she plays for the boys' team.*

Ever since he could see over the boards, Jack had watched Becca in goal. Even then, he realized how good she was in front of the net. She could stop anything.

Now, Becca was a sixteen-year-old girl on the boys high school team, and Jack was getting tired of answering questions about her.

He wanted to watch from the ice, not from the boards. He wanted to stand out on his own. Jack was confident this year would be different. His sister was a goalie. He was a center. They both could be great players in their own way, and he intended to prove it.

Tryouts for the AAA Peewee team were about two months away. Jack hoped if he worked hard enough, he could make the team as a sixth grader.

WHEEE! WHEEE!

Coach Vorwald's whistle refocused Jack's attention. The coach tossed red jerseys to a handful of players, including Jack.

"Scrimmage time," said Coach Vorwald. "Red versus green. We're going to practice some dump and chase. Centers, Jack and Mason, I'll dump to the corner. Players, take your places."

Coach Vorwald dropped the puck, but there was no face-off in this drill. The puck landed with a thwack on the ice. Coach Vorwald turned and dumped it into the red team's offensive end. Jack and Mason raced to reach it first.

Mason used to be one of Jack's best friends. He was a good center but an even better winger. The boys started out in Mites together and had been on teams together ever since. Mason had Jack beat on speed, but he couldn't match Jack's stickhandling.

Lately, Mason and Jack hadn't been seeing eye-to-eye when it came to hockey. Mason had talent but had started to get lazy and take shortcuts. He'd sometimes hang back and hope to get a loose puck instead of jumping into the play. He would try a slap shot from the corner instead of passing.

Jack was bothered by Mason's new style of play. Mason was cherry-picking.

Speed was speed, though, and Mason got to the puck that Coach Vorwald had dumped a second before Jack did. Jack caught up and was able to knock it away and get control.

He shot the puck out to one of the red team's defensemen and raced to the crease. The defenseman tapped it back. Jack deked Mason and tapped the puck through the goalie's five-hole for a sweet goal.

I'm Jack Wickman, thought Jack. *Not Becca Wickman's little brother.*

CHAPTER 2

REALITY CHECK

The next day, Jack walked into school. In the lobby, a wall was painted to read *Home of the Warriors*. Someone had hung a life-sized poster of his sister. It read: *OUR #1 WARRIOR*. The poster put Jack in the dumps.

Megan and Brooke, hockey players from the girls' Bantam team and friends of Jack, walked up. They stood next to Jack. The three of them gazed up at the poster.

"Pretty cool, huh?" said Brooke.

"Uh, I don't know," said Jack. "It might be too . . . big."

"I saw your sister's game," Megan said.

"Dude, she's awesome," added Brooke. "I bet she goes pro."

"Maybe," said Jack. He shoved his hands in his hoodie pockets.

"Dude, what's it feel like to live with a superstar?" Brooke asked.

"Super-duper," Jack replied.

Megan and Brooke laughed, not picking up on Jack's mood.

"Do you think she'll start on Friday?" Megan asked.

Jack shrugged. "We don't really have much time to talk during the season." he said. "Our game schedules and practice times are really busy. I have a game tomorrow, so I'm trying to concentrate on that."

Megan and Brooke stared at Jack.

"How can you not talk about hockey when you have a star in your house?" Megan asked. Her mouth remained open in disbelief.

"Dude," Brooke whispered. She placed her pointer finger under Megan's chin and slowly closed Megan's mouth for her.

Before Jack had a chance to respond, Brooke chimed in, asking, "Will your sister be at your game? Do you think that I can talk to her about hockey?"

The bell rang, saving Jack from having to answer. He grabbed his backpack and headed toward class.

"Hey!" Megan called. "Want to practice some shots after school? Your mom's place?"

Jack turned, gave a thumbs-up, and then continued on toward class. He heard hurried footsteps behind him.

"Hey," Mason said. "Fifty-seven days."

"Yeah?" Jack said. He was confused.

"Until tryouts?" Mason said. "Man, Wickman. Get your head in the game."

Jack knew there'd be competition for the AAA Peewee spot, but he hadn't guessed Mason would try out. Mason's natural ability gave him a good chance to make it. But his recent bad habits . . .

The boys entered a classroom and sat.

Mason dropped his backpack on the desk behind Jack. "Nice poster of your sister, by the way," Mason said. "I bet it feels familiar."

"What do you mean?" Jack asked.

Mason laughed. "Your sister being number one. You being number two."

Jack shook his head. It was a dumb comment. He pretended it didn't bother him.

CHAPTER 3

DRY LAND

Jack's mom lived in an apartment. In the parking lot, the landlord, Mr. Bakker, let the kids put a net up against the storage shed. Surrounding the net, black streaks and dents from poorly aimed pucks marked the side of the shed. Bakker likely knew he would have even more damage if he didn't have an area for the kids to practice.

With Mason competing for the AAA spot, Jack needed every spare moment he had to work on his skills. He planned on putting a few more dents in Bakker's shed.

Wearing full goalie gear except for the skates, Megan leaned against the lumber in the net. She lowered her facemask and then shuffled back and forth.

Jack carried a five-gallon pail of pucks. He dumped them on the ground in front of the net. That's where Megan was dropping to her knees to stop pretend pucks from getting into the goal. Jack picked up his stick and tapped a puck back and forth, moving it in front of Megan.

"So what's up?" Megan asked.

"What do you mean?" Jack replied.

"You're off your game," she said. "What's going on?"

Jack shot the puck in front of him toward the net. Megan stopped it with her blocker pad. She did a victory fist pump.

Jack spun his stick and slid another puck in front of him. This time he tapped the puck to his right and used a backhand to shoot toward the upper corner of the net.

Megan easily gloved the puck and then tossed it back to Jack. She did a second fist pump. This time she combined it with a dance move.

"Stop," Jack said. He tried not to smile.

Grabbing a different puck, Jack stepped away from the net. Megan had never shut him out on dry land practices.

Jack tapped his stick on the side of the puck, moving the puck to his left. He tapped on the opposite side of the puck and moved it to his right. Megan shuffled in the net, mirroring each move Jack made.

Jack slid the puck closer to the net. He lifted a quick wrist shot to the lower corner. Megan dropped to her knees and wedged her foot against the post. The puck bounced off her leg pad and rolled back toward Jack.

"Yooooooo!" Megan sang as she dropped her stick and did a full victory dance.

Jack couldn't help but laugh. "Okay," he said. "I give up."

Megan smiled. "Now, what was going on with you today?"

Jack stared at the ground and moved a puck with the toe of his shoe. "Sometimes, I get tired of people asking about Becca," Jack said. "I mean, I'm proud of her, but I skate too."

Megan picked at the tape on her stick and said, "Oh *noooooo*. The green-eyed monster."

"What?" Jack asked.

"It's my mom's saying for when someone is jealous," Megan said.

"Why?" Jack asked.

"No idea," said Megan. She shrugged. "But are you jealous?"

"Maybe," said Jack.

Megan took off her glove and wiped the sweat off her hand. She said, "You should have her back."

Megan's comment surprised Jack. Did people think he didn't have his sister's back? *Did* he have her back?

Jack slid a puck from the pile.

Megan put on her glove, squared to the puck, and relaxed her shoulders. "Just sayin', you know," she said.

Jack pulled back his stick and aimed high. When the puck zipped past Megan and pinged off the post and bounced in, Jack whooped. Then he dropped his stick and pumped his fist as Megan began to laugh.

CHAPTER 4

GAME DAY

Jack was happy to be back on the ice. Not only that, but two of the coaches from the AAA Peewee team were in the stands. The extra practice with Megan was paying off, and Jack was ready to show off his skill.

The buzzer sounded to end warm-ups. The pucks were cleared from the ice. All players except the starting lines skated to the bench.

Jack skated to center ice. The green and gold of his Warriors jersey stood out against the bright white of the rink.

The opposing center was a thick kid in sport goggles who wore a red and black Jaguars jersey. He smiled at Jack and said, "Good luck."

Jack didn't know if he meant it or not.

A referee stood at center ice with a puck behind his back. The other players got into position. The ref signaled for Jack and the goggled center to prepare for the face-off. Jack leaned forward and lowered the blade of his stick onto the ice.

The whistle blew, and Jack fought for the puck. He won the face-off and knocked the puck into the defensive end to gain control. Jack skated toward the net as the two Warriors defensemen passed it back and forth along the blue line.

One of the players dumped the puck around the boards. Jack raced ahead of the opposing center and got to the puck first. Behind the net, Jack lost control when the Jaguars center reached him and blocked the puck between his skates.

Jack pushed himself between the center and the boards. The Jaguars center jabbed at the puck with his stick. Knocking the puck free, Jack was able to pass it to a Warrior waiting near the crease.

The winger backhanded the puck toward the goal's lower right corner, but the goalie gloved the puck. The referee blew the whistle, stopping play.

Jack readied for the next face-off. The referee waited for the players to line up. The goggled center moved forward over the hash marks.

"Square up," the ref said.

The Jaguars center backed up. The ref dropped the puck. Jack lost this time, and a Jaguars defenseman shot the puck into the neutral zone. A Jaguars winger batted the puck into the Warriors defensive end.

It was a two-on-one race to the goal. Elijah, the Warriors goalie, skated out to cut off the angle.

The Jaguars center shot the puck. The puck hit Elijah's leg pad and slid just out of the goal crease. Jack chased the play. He saw a Warriors defenseman out of position and raced to help Elijah.

The Jaguars center got his stick on the puck and shot before Elijah had a chance to recover. The puck went into the back of the net for a goal.

The Jaguars took the lead, 1–0.

The number one lit up in red under the GUEST side of the scoreboard. Jack looked up in the stands and saw his mom, dad, and sister watching the scoreboard. The two AAA coaches watched Jack for his reaction.

Jack whacked his stick against his shin pad. He skated to center ice and leaned forward with his stick across his knees. After the face-off, which he won, Jack hurried off ice for a shift change. He plopped down onto the bench.

Twice Jack watched as Mason had a chance to pass for a goal but took a shot instead. A third time, Mason waited at the blue line rather than going after the puck.

Mason wasn't the Warriors' only problem. As Jack watched, he saw skaters not covering on defense and wingers not helping out in the corners. Jack knew the Warriors had a tough climb ahead if they hoped to beat the Jaguars.

Coach Vorwald noticed the problems too. He signaled the players to huddle up between the second and third period.

"What's going on, guys?" Coach Vorwald yelled. "It's like you've never played together before. You're not covering the points. You're not hustling. Get it together!"

Some of the guys dropped their heads.

Coach Vorwald wasn't finished. "Mason," he said, "stop hanging back. The only good thing that happens at the blue line is a breakaway."

Coach continued, "Move your legs. Jack, shake off the goal. How about we see a little of your sister's toughness out there?"

Jack slouched lower on the bench.

"Hands in," Coach Vorwald said.

Coach Vorwald threw his hand out. Each player reached into the circle with a glove.

"Team on three," Coach Vorwald said. "One, two . . ."

The Warriors shouted, "Team!"

By the end of the third period, the scolding didn't matter. Both Jack and Coach Vorwald had been proven right. The game was still 1–0. Time was running out.

Play was stopped with one minute remaining on the clock.

As Mason skated to the bench, Jack called to him. "Mason, you have to pass sometimes," said Jack. "Don't be such a puck hog."

"You're not my coach," Mason said. The face-off was in the offensive end, and it was Jack's shift. His last chance.

Jack knew that the Jaguars goalie was a leftie. If Jack could get the puck out to the opposite side of the net, a winger might have the chance to tip it in.

The referee dropped the puck. Jack fought for it and got his stick on it. He tapped it to a Warriors winger.

The goal was open on the right side, and the winger took a shot. The goalie read the play, dropped to butterfly position, and blocked the attempt. A Jaguars defenseman scooped the puck and iced it to the opposite end of the rink.

Jack skated for the puck, but the buzzer sounded. The noise ended the game and ended Jack's hope for a big win. Jack looked up in the stands. The AAA coaches had already left the rink.

As Jack stepped off the ice, Becca was at the rink door. Jack shook his head when he saw her and walked in the opposite direction toward the locker room door.

CHAPTER 5

PIZZA AND SKEE-BALL

After the Warriors' loss, Jack shoved his gear in his hockey bag and headed off to find his dad, who stood waiting in the hallway. Mason waited next to Jack's dad. Seeing Mason stopped Jack in his tracks.

Jack thought about Mason's play on the ice. Jack realized he was still angry at Mason. Mason's scowl said he wasn't happy to see Jack, either.

"What's up?" Jack asked.

"Mason needs a ride home," said Jack's dad.

Jack slung his bag over his shoulder. He looked down directly at the floor as he walked past his teammate.

"You guys hungry?" Jack's dad asked.

It was still early for a Saturday, and Jack was starving. But he shook his head. Jack didn't care to spend time with Mason.

"Starving," Mason replied.

"Luigi's?" Jack's dad suggested, ignoring Jack. Luigi's was the local pizza place. It was also Jack's favorite restaurant, mostly because of the awesome arcade.

"Sweet!" Mason said.

"I guess," Jack replied.

They rode to Luigi's in awkward silence.

When they arrived, Jack's dad said, "Pizza, then Skee-Ball." He dug quarters out of the cup holder in his car and gave the boys a handful of change.

Jack and Mason hurried inside.

As they sat together eating, Jack stuffed himself with pizza and mostly avoided talking. Afterward, they lined up quarters on the Skee-Ball machine.

"Highest score gets to pick dessert," said Jack's dad, dropping a quarter into the game. Nine balls rolled down the narrow wooden ramp. He rolled his first ball into the 100-point hole. After nine throws, he had scored 270 points.

Jack threw next. His first throw made the 50-point ring. After that, though, he seemed doomed to hit only the 10-point ring. Jack's final score was a low 130 points.

Mason threw last. His first three throws ended up in the 10-point rings.

"Playing it safe, Mason?" Jack's dad joked.

Mason laughed.

"Just like hockey," Jack said. "Mason finds the easiest way to score."

Mason pretended to laugh again, but Jack's dad stared at Jack. His dad was a relaxed guy, but he didn't put up with rudeness.

"Really hate to break it to you, pal," Jack's dad said, "but you weren't that hot on the ice today, either."

Jack's face went red.

"I think you owe Mason an apology," Jack's dad added.

Jack swallowed and coughed. "Sorry, Mason," he managed to mumble.

"I don't think I'm up for dessert," Jack's Dad said. "Becca's game starts soon anyway."

Mason stared at Jack. He dropped the Skee-Ball, not finishing his turn.

CHAPTER 6

SHOOTING STAR

Jack sat alone at the rink. He watched from the stands as Becca worked the ice in front of the net. Over his shoulder, Jack saw Mason joke with a few Warriors teammates. Jack's dad stood at the top of the bleachers by himself, watching Becca.

Jack focused back on Becca. He watched as she blocked warm-up shots taken by her Warriors teammates. Once, a longhaired defenseman hit a slap shot at the same time as another Warriors skater. The puck came in high and bounced off Becca's helmet.

Becca dropped her stick and skated toward the longhaired kid. Jack could tell that she was angry.

Jack couldn't hear what was said, but he knew that it was heated. The longhaired kid had taken a cheap shot for some reason. *Maybe*, Jack thought, *just because she was a girl.* It made Jack angry.

Several of Becca's teammates joined her. One got between the longhaired kid and Becca and shoved the kid. Becca glared at the kid as she picked up her stick and returned to the net.

Jack thought about how most of Becca's team seemed to have her back. *Teamwork,* Jack thought, *just add it to the list of things Becca does better than me.*

Back in the net, Becca squared up. The pucks came toward her again. She stopped nearly all of them. Clearly, Becca had a gift.

After a while, Megan and Brooke joined Jack in the stands.

"Hey, how'd the game go?" Brooke asked.

Jack shrugged.

"I heard Elijah had 27 saves. Dude, that's awesome," Brooke said. "What was the final?"

"We lost, one to nothing," Jack said.

"Bummer," Megan said. "So why aren't you hanging out with the team?"

Jack's shoulders slumped. He was too embarrassed to tell Megan the truth. His face turned red. "I don't know," Jack said.

Megan looked at Brooke. Brooke looked back at Megan. They both looked at Jack. The game soon began.

Midway through the first period, the game was scoreless. The Warriors' opponent, the Panthers, had been coming at Becca hard, and now a Panthers winger took another shot on goal.

Becca blocked it, and it deflected away.

Another Panthers skater swung at the puck.

Becca blocked this shot too and tried to cover the puck, but just then, the longhaired Warriors player slid into the crease. Clumsily, he knocked the puck loose in front of the net. The Panthers center quickly tapped it past Becca, who looked behind her for the puck.

Too late. Goal.

Jack's eyes widened. It should have been an easy save. Megan and Brooke hung their heads. Becca looked at the ceiling in disbelief.

As the game continued, the aggressive play was nonstop. The Panthers took shot after shot, and Becca stopped them all. All but one. By the end of the game, shots on goal were 37 to 21. Like Jack's Warriors, Becca's Warriors lost, 1–0.

Becca skated to center ice to congratulate the opposing goalie. Then she skated back to the net. She seemed calm until she smacked her stick against the post. Jack wasn't the only family member who didn't like to lose. He hurried down to meet his sister, the metal stands clanking. Megan and Brooke followed.

Mason brushed by Jack. "Guess the Wickman family is zero for two," said Mason.

"What's your problem, Mason?" Jack said.

Mason glanced at Becca, who was watching the boys from behind the glass.

"Never mind," Mason said. "It looks like big sister is coming to the rescue."

Jack stepped forward and clenched his fists. He was ready to go at Mason.

Megan hopped between the two boys. "Dudes!" she said. "Don't."

CHAPTER 7

TEAMWORK?

"Something going on with your team?" Becca asked on the ride home with their dad.

"What? No," Jack lied.

Jack's dad threw a sideways glance at him.

"Is Mason bothering you?" Becca asked.

"No," Jack said.

"It's a really important year for me," Becca said. "I can't worry about you all the time."

For the third time that day, Jack felt angry. "It's a big year for me too," Jack said. "Maybe you should spend less time worrying about me and more time trying not to lose."

"That's enough," Jack's dad said. "Talk to each other when you can be respectful."

They rode the rest of the way home in silence. They ate dinner in silence. They went to bed in silence. Jack fell asleep that night without saying another word to his sister.

The next morning, both the anger and the loss hung over Jack's head. He wondered if he'd ruined his chances of making the AAA Peewee team. He wondered when his sister would talk to him. He wondered what would happen when he saw Mason.

Jack now knew that he needed to work on more than his hockey. He just wasn't sure how to fix the issues he was having with friends, so he dove into the game. With AAA tryouts coming in just a few weeks, Jack practiced nightly. When he couldn't be on the ice, he practiced dry-land shots and worked out. To help his son build up leg muscle, Jack's dad had built a homemade slide board.

The board was a long and smooth ramp with deep edges. Jack would put on fuzzy socks and push himself side to side on the ramp. The slide board let him "skate" at home for more practice. The extra workouts helped. Jack felt himself beginning to catch up with Mason's speed.

One practice, while doing one of Coach Vorwald's speed drills, Jack beat Mason for the very first time. It was the first time Mason's talent wasn't enough.

Near the end of that same practice, Coach Vorwald called for a quick scrimmage. Ice time for the varsity team started next, so a few of the older boys were watching through the glass. Becca stood next to her teammates.

"Becca!" Coach Vorwald yelled. "Cover the other end."

Becca put on her helmet, stepped on the ice, and skated to the open net. Coach Vorwald threw red or green mesh jerseys to every other player. Mason was red. Jack was green.

"Becca's on the red team," Coach said.

Becca tightened her chinstrap. When she nodded, Coach Vorwald skated to center ice. Mason and Jack faced one another and readied. Coach Vorwald dropped the puck.

The scrimmage was chippy from the start. Jack and Mason shoved each other out of the face-off. When Mason passed the puck to a defenseman, Jack checked him from behind, nearly knocking him off his feet. Mason's team regained control and passed to center ice. Jack blocked the pass. He stalled in the neutral zone to avoid an offsides call.

"Looking weak, Wickman," Mason said. He hip-checked Jack into the boards.

"Need another speed drill?"Jack replied.

Jack managed to slap the puck into the offensive zone. Mason took control. Jack chased Mason into the corner.

Becca hugged the post, watching them battle.

Fighting for the puck, Mason and Jack jostled for position. Jack knocked the puck free from the corner. He tapped it to the crease.

Becca dropped to cover the puck. As she did, Mason ran into Jack from behind. Jack shoved Mason and accidentally elbowed Becca.

Becca fell backward onto the ice. Regaining her feet, she spit out her mouthguard. "You guys having fun?" she said. "'Cause I'm not."

Coach Vorwald blew the whistle. "Jack, Mason, locker room," he said. "You're done for the day."

CHAPTER 8
BREAKING AWAY

It was the last game before tryouts, and Jack was running out of friends. Mason wasn't speaking to him. Becca was still mad. Megan and Brooke were being cold since he and Mason had nearly fought at the rink. It was a mess.

Jack had never played better or felt worse. Before the game, Jack and Mason sat across from each other in the locker room. Their teammates laughed and chatted. Mason laced up his skates. Jack taped his stick.

When it was time to warm up, the team filed out of the locker room and into the rink. Becca, Megan, Brooke, and Jack's dad watched from the stands. Jack knew he would need to try hard to focus on the game.

For the past week, Coach Vorwald had made both Jack and Mason skate laps every day after practice for the elbow to Becca. Coach probably hoped the two would work it out. They hadn't.

The opposing team, the Rebels, wore purple and white. After warm-ups, the bench players hopped the boards to take a seat while the starting lines huddled one last time.

The Warriors starters skated to center ice. Jack cleared his head. He took his spot in the face-off circle. The Rebels starting center, a guy with braces but no mouthguard, faced off against Jack.

The Rebels center won the face-off and was able to dump the puck. Jack back-checked hard and hustled toward the play. The braces kid and a Warriors grinder fought for the puck in the corner.

A Warriors defenseman dumped the puck into the neutral zone. Jack chased the puck for a blue line breakaway.

He would have a one-on-one showdown with the goalie if he hustled. The braces skater tried to catch up.

Jack dangled the puck and waited for his chance. When the goalie opened his legs, Jack flicked the puck with a light touch. The puck shot through the goalie's legs for a five-hole score.

GOAL!

Jack high-fived a Warriors defenseman. From the cheering crowd, Becca and Jack's dad gave Jack a thumbs-up. Except for Mason, all the Warriors, including Coach Vorwald, were pumped up.

Jack won the next face-off again and dumped the puck down ice. He hurried to the bench for a shift change. Mason hopped the boards to the ice. The puck whizzed past Mason. A Rebels winger and Mason got tangled up. Mason went head over skates.

Mason's gloves, stick, and mouthguard scattered across the ice. It looked like a yard sale.

The referee blew the whistle, stopping the play. Mason gathered up his things and skated to the bench.

The third-line center hustled onto the ice for Mason, and Mason sat next to Jack on the bench.

"You okay?" Jack asked.

"That," Mason said, "was embarrassing." He slid down the bench away from Jack.

The Rebels and Warriors were evenly matched. After two periods, the Warriors still held a 1–0 lead. During a third period break on the bench, Jack realized that he wasn't the only one who had improved. His teammates were all getting better.

That included Mason, who was digging in the corners and actually hustling. The Warriors got their second goal of the game thanks to Mason. He faked a shot and froze the goalie before passing it to a teammate, who scored.

The game ended with a hard-fought 2–0 Warriors win. Jack knew he was ready for Peewee tryouts. But he still felt like something was off.

CHAPTER 9

IN THE ZONE

After the game, some of the players went to Luigi's to celebrate. Jack wanted to go home.

Their dad drove Jack and Becca as the two sat next to one another in silence.

"Remember when I said I can't worry about you this year?" Becca asked.

"Yeah," Jack said.

"I'm worried," Becca said.

"Yeah," Jack replied and dropped his shoulders. "I've been a jerk. I'm sorry, Becca." Jack looked at his sister. "Are we good now?" he asked.

"We're good," Becca said.

Becca smiled. Jack knew he was forgiven.

"Any idea how I make it right with my friends?" Jack asked.

Becca thought for a moment. "I think I might," Becca answered.

***

The next day after school, Jack felt more nervous about seeing his friends than he had been for the game. He and Becca had come up with a plan. Jack asked Becca to invite Megan, Brooke, and Mason over to the apartment. Jack knew they would have a hard time saying no to his sister.

Megan, Brooke, and Mason met Jack out by Bakker's practice shed. When they arrived, Becca awaited them in full goalie gear, in the net.

Becca looked at the group and asked, "May I practice with you?"

Megan, Brooke, and Mason stared at Jack wide-eyed.

"I've been a jerk," Jack said.

"Totally," Megan said.

"A major jerk," Brooke said.

Mason looked at the ground. "I may have been part of the problem," Mason said.

"*May* have?" Megan asked.

"Dude," Brooke said to Mason.

"OK. I am part of the problem," Mason said. "Sorry, Jack."

"Me too," Jack said.

"Ugh, are we done apologizing?" Becca asked. "Are we going to practice or what?"

Megan, Brooke, and Mason whooped and hollered. Becca invited Megan into the net to give her some pointers.

Mason, Brooke, and Jack passed back and forth. After Megan was warmed up, the others took shots.

"Move forward to cut off the angle," Becca said to Megan. "It makes it harder to score."

Megan took a step forward into the crease and caught the next shot in her glove.

"Nice," Becca said.

Mason and Jack practiced passing back and forth. Brooke kept firing shots at Megan.

Becca stepped into the net.

"Your turn, Jack-O'-Lantern," Becca said.

"What?" Megan asked.

"Did?" Brooke asked.

"She?" Mason asked.

"Yes," Jack said, laughing. "She called me Jack-O'-Lantern."

"*Awwwww,*" the group said all at once.

"Yeah, yeah," Jack said. He scooped a pile of pucks toward him and prepared to shoot.

"Line up your shot, Superstar. Or do you prefer Hot Shot?" Becca asked.

Oh, it was on. Jack lined up the puck as if he was ready to shoot.

Becca got into position. "Where would you shoot?" she asked.

"Top corner," Jack said.

"Now, get down on the ground and look at the net from the puck," Becca said.

Megan, Mason, Brooke, and Jack took turns getting down to look up from the puck.

"Now where would you shoot?" Becca asked.

"Probably between your blocker and leg," Jack said. The others nodded in agreement.

"Where do you look?" Megan asked Becca.

Becca said, "Always at the puck, but sometimes at the ice in front of the stick. Almost never at the player."

Megan nodded.

Each player took turns shooting on Becca, but none even got close to the net. They practiced for more than an hour. They were having so much fun, no one noticed the time. Jack's mom approached the group and said it was time to call it a night.

"Two more minutes?" Becca asked.

Jack's mom zipped her coat and watched them continue to shoot.

Jack lined up his final shot for the night and tried to imagine what the shot looked like from the ground. Jack pulled back his stick and lowered his grip.

He brought down his stick with all of his power. The flat of his blade connected with the puck. It was the fastest slap shot he'd ever hit.

His mouth dropped open when he realized the puck made it into the net. Becca threw up her arms in celebration, and the entire group cheered. Mason punched Jack's shoulder, and Brooke patted his back. Megan tossed her gloves into the air.

"That's what I'm talking about!" Becca said.

"Thanks, Chew-Becca," Jack said.

"Did?" Megan asked.

"He?" Brooke asked.

"Say?" Mason asked.

"Yes," Becca said.

"*Awwwwww*," the group said all together.

CHAPTER 10

AAA DAY

Tryouts. Just two spots open on the AAA team. More than fifty kids took the ice with several adults watching them play.

The skaters were divided into groups of ten and started with skating drills. After the drills, the coaches added pucks to judge the players' stickhandling skills. Jack handled the drills with ease. Mason occasionally let a puck get away from him but always seemed to recover.

Finally, the coaches set up four-on-four plays. Again, Jack and Mason were paired up. Jack was happy they had a chance to work together on the ice. During the scrimmage, Jack played as center and Mason played as winger. The two passed easily back and forth.

Not once did Mason slow at the blue line. Instead Mason pushed past a defenseman and shot the puck around the boards.

The other winger player was able to pick up the puck and send it into the slot where Jack was waiting. Jack looked for an opening and shot toward the five-hole. The goalie dropped into butterfly position, but it was too late. The puck was in the net!

Mason patted Jack's helmet. "Good job," Mason said. He smiled.

"Thanks," Jack said. He felt relieved and happy. "Nice pass."

The coaches took the puck back to center ice and whistled to start play again. Tryouts lasted about an hour. Jack left the ice tired. He'd done his best.

***

A few days later, Jack made his way to the rink after school let out. The list for the AAA team would be taped next to the door at the rink. Becca's game was about to start, and he wanted to see the results before the game.

Jack walked into the lobby. The entryway was mostly empty, except for Becca. She stood in her game gear next to the tryout list.

She smiled and pointed to Mason's name on the AAA team. Then she beamed as she moved her finger up the list to Jack's name.

"You know, I didn't make the AAA team until the seventh grade," Becca said.

Jack's eyes widened. "No way," he said.

"Nice job, Wickman," Becca said, checking Jack with her shoulder.

"Thanks, Becca," Jack said, following his sister into the rink.

AUTHOR BIO

Melissa Brandt has written a number of feature-length screenplays and was awarded the 2012 McKnight Fellowship for her screenplay called *Chicken Day*. She grew up in Worthington, Minnesota, and now lives in Rochester, Minnesota, with her hockey-playing and hockey-loving family.

ILLUSTRATOR BIO

Sean Tiffany has worked in the illustration and comic book field for more than twenty years. He has illustrated more than sixty children's books for Capstone and has been an instructor at the famed Joe Kubert School in northern New Jersey. Raised on a small island off the coast of Maine, Sean now resides in Boulder, Colorado, with his wife, Monika, their son, James, a cactus named Jim, and a room

HOCKEY GLOSSARY

blocker—the goaltender's padded glove that goes on the hand that holds the stick

blue line—either of the two blue-colored lines running across the ice between the center line and the goal line

butterfly position—move made by a goaltender when extending both legs in opposite directions in order to stop a low shot

center—the main forward position in hockey

check—a sudden stopping of forward motion; in hockey, it involves one player slamming into another

cherry-pick—to stay near center ice hoping to pick up a breakout pass with no defenders in the way instead of helping out the team on defense

chippy—aggressive, rough play in hockey

crease—semi-circular area in front of each goal; where no offensive players are allowed when a goal is scored

deke—shortened form of the word "decoy"; involves faking with the puck to confuse a defender or goalie

five-hole—the area between the goaltender's legs

neutral zone—the middle part of an ice hockey rink between the two blue lines

wing—the secondary forward position in hockey

DISCUSSION QUESTIONS

1. What are the ways you can tell that Jack looks up to his sister, Becca? If there's someone you look up to in the same way, who is it and why do you admire them?

2. When Jack is playing Skee-Ball with his dad and Mason, he says something rude to Mason. Why do you think Jack's dad reacted the way he did to his son's comment?

3. On the final page of the story, we find out that both Jack and Mason made the AAA team. What's an opportunity or experience you would love to be able to share with a friend? Why?

WRITING PROMPTS

1. Early in the story, Jack is envious of his sister's success. Admiration (looking up to someone for their positive qualities) can be useful, but jealousy is usually destructive. Write about a time you felt either of those feelings about someone in your life.

2. Imagine Jack's first day of AAA practice. Write a scene where something great or terrible happens and how Jack handles it.

3. Try writing a poem about hockey. Use hockey words from the glossary in this book like *blue line, butterfly position, cherry picker, deke, and neutral zone.*

MORE ABOUT HOCKEY

Some historians believe hockey was invented in Canada. Others believe the sport got its start in Britain in the 1790s.

When a player scores three goals in a game, it's called a hat trick. If the player scores three goals in a row, without anyone scoring in-between, it's called a natural hat trick.

Eveleth, Minnesota, is home to the United States Hockey Hall of Fame.

The best-known professional hockey league, the National Hockey League (NHL), was founded in 1917.

The Montreal Canadiens have won 23 championships, the most in NHL history.

The championship trophy given in the NHL is called the Stanley Cup. It was first awarded in 1892 and is the oldest trophy given in major sports.

The Stanley Cup is named after Frederick Stanley, a man who was born in London, England, and went on to become the Governor General of Canada.